Hi! I'm Sol.
Hi! I'm Kit!

Sol, Kit and Ben
begin to get fed up.

But it can be so …
so … dull on a rocket.

So the cabin is set up for a football game.

Kick it, Sol!
Yes!! It's a goal! 1–0!

But Kit can kick well too! She kicks the ball low into the net!

But back on Earth the big game is on ...

On a rocket ...
... we can still be ...
... on the ball!